SHOOTOUT
WITH
FATHER

SHOOTOUT
WITH
FATHER

**MARIANNE
HAUSER**

FC2
Normal/Tallahassee

Published by FC2 with support provided by Florida State University, the Unit for Contemporary Literature of the Department of English at Illinois State University, the Program for Writers of the Department of English of the University of Illinois at Chicago, the Illinois Arts Council, and the Florida Arts Council of the Florida Division of Cultural Affairs

Address all inquiries to: Fiction Collective Two, Florida State University, c/o English Department, Tallahassee, FL 32306-1580

ISBN: Paper, 1-57366-100-7

Library of Congress Cataloging-in Publication Data

Hauser, Marianne.
    Shootout with father / Marianne Hauser.-- 1st ed.
        p. cm.
    ISBN 1-57366-100-7
    1. Fathers and sons--Fiction. 2. Armor--Collectors and collecting--Fiction. 3. Parent and adult child--Fiction. 4. New York (N.Y.)--Fiction. 5. Businessmen--Fiction. 6. Artists--Fiction. I. Title.
    PS3558.A7587 S56 2002
    813'.54--dc21

                                        2001006710

Cover Design: Victor Mingovits
Book Design: Tara Reeser

Produced and printed in the United States of America
Printed on recycled paper with soy ink

This program is partially supported by a grant from the Illinois Arts Council

This story is for
Robert Beers

Minutes before closing time my old man appears at the gallery. Now that he is technically blind, he condescends to see my show. With measured steps he enters on the arm of his lady companion or seeing eye, his custom-made tweeds too loose on his aged frame, his shoulders stooped. But his commanding presence remains undiminished. An air of power and money shields him like an armor. Old power. Old money. You can smell it miles away.

His eyes are hidden behind shades. Yet I could swear he has them trained on me. Abruptly he's pulled free from the arm of his fur-swathed companion. Well then, shall we take a shot at it, Mrs. Q? His voice is raspy. He turns his head this way and that as if to appraise the market value of the gallery space. Then he snaps his fingers twice. Shall we have a look at my son's...er...objets d'art? But first we must greet the artist. Where would he be hiding?

●

Hiding. I wish I could. Again he's got me by the balls, the old bastard. Now that he sees no more than an occasional flash of light, he'll have a look at what he maliciously refers to as his son's objets d'art. Mind you, not objets trouvés. Not even junk. That would lend distinction as cult art to my small sculptures. And the la-di-da lilt he affects as he pronounces the French.... It's a studied provocation for which I ought to be prepared and never am. Each time I'm stung anew. Each time he wins.

•

And yet.... The mere fact that he took the trouble to come to the opening... I'm grateful, damn it. I'm moved. For years I've mailed him an invitation. He never responded. Still, I continued the charade—why? Surely not because I'm after his money. Mother has left me plenty. No, those announcements I sent him (with a rather groveling note attached) had become a ritual, as our whole relationship is in fact ritualistic, managed from a safe distance. When he needs to get in touch, he will dictate a letter to his secretary. "Dear son" etcetera. A typed communication, with "Father" penned in a thick scrawl across "Sincerely yours." Not a hint of affection. Since Mother's death the formality has somewhat lessened. But there's no warmth. None.

You may rightly ask why I don't just ignore the bastard. But ah! that is impossible. Nobody can ignore him, least of all I. He is unique, a genius not only in corporate business deals, but as a collector of ancient armor. The subterranean armory in the old family house glares, rattles and threatens with steely warriors who in my childhood scared me half to death. What former friend suggested I was working with metal to build my own miniature armory?

No matter. Father has come to my opening. His acknowledgment that I exist at all as an artist, albeit one without name or fame, flatters the pants off me. You'd be amazed how low a character like me can sink. A few hasty swigs from the flask, and I rush forth to kiss his ass.

Thank you for coming, Father!

•

Gummed eyes searching the shadow walls of my loft. Jittery hand searching blindly for the bottle. And all at once I realize that I'm still in the clothes I wore at the gallery. Must have passed out on my bed, too far gone to shed the formal suit. Was it for Mother's funeral that I last wore it?

The coat sits on my chest like armor; and struggling out of it, I hear the crash or clash not of steel but of glass as the bottle topples and breaks on the floor. There goes the rest of the vodka. And today is the day of the lord and every liquor store in the city is closed and shuttered.

I morosely stare at the bottle shards in a smell of spilled booze—the nostalgic smell of old saloons, I think, trying to stop the hangover shakes as I set about to clean up the mess.

•

So what keeps him from running downstairs to the nearest saloon? you'll ask. But I don't dare to, not since last night after the cursed opening when I got so smashed at the neighborhood bar I lost all judgment; buying round after round for the cheering gang; proclaiming a wizened wino my buddy for life; and finally, with drunk aplomb, smacking a wad of large bills on the bar top: Help yourself, gentlemen! (The saloon did not welcome ladies.)

From here on memory turns mute, up to the sudden nightmare when I came to in a patrol car, squeezed in between a pair of burly cops. Fortunately I am white. And I had my credentials on me. Not that my cheap downtown address would have cleared me of I still have no idea what crime. It was my almighty father who came to my rescue by proxy. When the cops had laboriously spelled out his residence from an engraved card in my depleted wallet, they all but saluted. They apologized profusely, and blamed a crack dealer on parole for giving them the bum steer. They drove me home, helped me up the stairs and kissed me good night. The latter may be read symbolically.

•

Thank god they didn't contact my old man! I'd rather not imagine the scene, had he got wind of my drunkenly squandering the sacred dollar I hadn't earned. Such shameless disposal of inherited wealth among the rabble would surely constitute the ultimate crime, one he neither could nor would allow himself to forgive, I ponder as I flop down again on the bed, the telephone close at hand while I watch the first snow of the season drive past the windows.

•

But this is becoming a winter habit, my slumping down on the bed, waiting—for what? A phone call from Mrs. Q? *Your daddy passed painlessly in his slumber.* Or a call from the great man himself? *Come over right away, my son. I am old and I need your love.*

The last scenario seems the most remote. I try in vain to picture it. Reality cuts me short. The tape whirs back to the gallery and freezes on Father's eyes, then unrolls in slow motion.

His eyes behind smoked window glass are trained on me, converging into a gun barrel. I'd like to have a closer look, Mrs. Q. Why don't you show me one of his things.

This time around it's things. She happens to pick my latest, a copper assemblage of seven triangles, spherical arcs mounted on a cut of black rock. What will the verdict be? I wait.

His shades reflect a toy-sized gallery as he turns to the piece she has lifted toward him to touch. But his hands stay locked behind his back.

I manage to open my mouth. She's showing you my most recent work. I finished it this past summer. On Clone.

Clone Island, North Carolina. Off the coast of the Outer Banks? Good fishing and hunting.

His hands have flown up from behind him and into the light. Finely shaped, sensitive hands. Who'd guess they would beat up on a seven year old for sobbing over a dead moose. The boy knee high in dry leaves and needles, bawling his lungs out: You killed him! You shot him dead! And the hands ripping the leather belt off the boy's pants to administer twelve strokes, precisely and fiercely, on the bare rump.

•

But at the gallery I didn't think of that episode in the northern woods, even though it has become a recurring nightmare as if he'd whipped me routinely, when he never laid a hand on me again. At the gallery my attention was caught up in the remarkable agility of his fingers as they sketched an invisible map into midair. Fish shaped Roanoke Island...the skinny branch of Hatteras stretching south between sound and sea...

...and here, my boy...(voice rising sharply, thumb plunging into the sea)...here you have Clone. Correct?

Correct, Father.

Indeed, he had with fair accuracy placed an obscure island and outlined a region I doubt he'd bother to visit. Our sort pass their summers down-east.

Or has he visited the island? Did he crouch behind a dune, watching me through a tremulant curtain of sea oats? Don't rule out anything with him. The man is a plethora of surprises.

•

An odd choice for spending your summers—since you don't fish. Or shoot!

I'd be violating the law if I did. Clone is a wildlife refuge.

I can't help grinning while he snaps at me that the entire nation would be a wildlife refuge if I and my muddle-headed comrades were running the show. What comrades? The birds and the beasts? But I shut up. Maybe it was a mistake to tell him about my yearly escape to Clone. Down there where sand and sea and sky melt into undefinable space in the heat, I'm out from under his shadow and free to assemble my dreams. Does he sense it, however vaguely?

I think he does. For now he starts to downgrade my poor Clone. Impossible accommodations. Black, biting flies and nasty climate. Unexpected, savage storms that whip the sea into mountainous waves and hurl the ships landward to smash on the beaches!

For five long centuries the narrow passage south around the shoals has been the dread of every sailor, my old man states sonorously. *The Graveyard of the Atlantic*. Isn't that what they call your region?

•

His voice echoed through the gallery—another graveyard. It was past closing time. The last stragglers had left. My dealer stood at an awed distance, hoping against hope she'd make a sale.

Spanish galleons, packed with gold from Mexico, wrecked on their passage home...wrecks scattered far and wide across the sand...

He paused, lost in the sixteenth century. Then he murmured absently: A boy on a treasure hunt.

He was that boy. His eyes behind the shades were looking inward. He was talking to himself and I was quick to pick up on cue, oh yes, the fury of the storms, they still blow in some treasures, when the worst is over I rush from my cabin and comb the beaches, I comb through huge tangles of seaweed and tar-stiffened rope, I crawl inside barnacled hulls to find my kind of treasure, the kind of copper I need for my assemblages, my work, Father.

My work. At last he reaches out and touches it. And as his fingertips begin to explore, carefully stroking each surface, curve, edge and angle, I ask myself in a surge of affection or sadness: would he make a better father if he had been born blind?

•

My ears still ring with the sudden click of his fingernails against thin metal. It's copper all right, he said. And lowering his head, he asked in the confidential tone of the versed collector to name him a price.

He was about to buy me! To own me! I was too moved to speak. I could only gape like an idiot while he repeated his question in the same secretive tone.

The price? Why, nothing! For you it's nothing, Father! I burst out. Please do accept it as a gift. (Would joyfully throw in the rest of the show. Would love to throw my arms around him if I dared. The man does have a heart!)

Come again? He bent an ear. A gift, you said? That's mighty generous, but you misheard. I've no intention to acquire or otherwise add to the excessive clutter of my home, unless (one eye seeming to wink at me through the dark lens), unless it so happens I chance across a rare find for my collection. In which case I'd be adding nothing new, of course, but something extremely ancient.

He chuckled and I felt the old hate rise from my guts, though I knew at once that under no circumstances must I give him the satisfaction to notice. Calm down. Act cool, I warned myself.

Too late, I'd lost control.

No need to explain, sir. I never presumed you'd waste your oh so precious money on my objets d'art. And adding that he'd obviously just been enjoying a joke at my expense, I had, to mix two relevant metaphors, signed my own death warrant at the flip of a coin.

A joke! Won't you ever grow up? The rejected gift was back in Mrs. Q's plump hands. I'd better get it into my thick skull that money was indeed a precious commodity. His asking for the price did by no means imply that he wished to buy and collect me as my mother had, the poor dear. No! He was simply curious how a downward trend in the art market showed in my sales figures.

I still am curious—well? How much? Or am I supposed to contact your dealer?

My dealer who charges me for the gallery space! I felt like laughing in his face. But I couldn't even force a sneer or a snub. I could only reply that my stuff, if it sold at all, sold cheap regardless of the ups and downs of a market which was a deep dark mystery to me in any case.

Bully for you, my boy. Few artists can afford such deep dark mysteries. I trust you can.

And with that ominous putdown or caveat my case was dismissed. He donned his overcoat, pulled the

17

collar up to his nose, and on the arm of Mrs. Q strode off into the deepfreeze night to his hearse. That's how I'd see his big black car at such black moments. Let's get cracking. I need my sleep. Can we give you a lift? Thank you, sir, but no. I'll walk. And so we split.

•

You know the finale, how I woke up in a stupor, without the faintest notion who or what had whisked me from my cozy neighborhood bar into a patrol car. Now as I lie in my hangover gloom, I hope to psych myself into a similar state of oblivion and black out last night's dismal confrontation. But I fail. No matter what tricks I employ—fixing my eyes on the soldering torch on the work table, or floating disembodied in the void— the demons beat me to it. The void fills with Father's chuckle. The soldering torch converts into a gun. My brain films what I mean to cut, as yesterday's plot repeats itself in myriad versions until the characters trade roles. He becomes me while I become my father.

•

Shoot the motherfucker!
I'm ranting through a wet dream. I stick the gun into my mouth and wake up. The phone is ringing. But as soon as I've wiped the cum off my fingers, the ringing stops.

18

Did I miss an urgent call from Mrs. Q, advising me of her boss' imminent passage to the beyond? Or a call from the boss himself: My son, come over right away. I am old and I need your love. Not bloody likely, Buster, I correct myself, borrowing from his repertoire of snarled comebacks.

•

Still snowing, and the afternoon is trapped in the same false twilight. I must have slept less than a minute. But the dream has dredged up what I'd rather leave buried—the real gun that Father gave me some months ago for my birthday. Not that he gave it to me in person. That's not his style. He sent his chauffeur up with it, the old man meanwhile waiting downstairs in the hearse. Or so I fancied. I didn't look.

A small pistol, bedded in an alligator case which I'd snapped open in naive anticipation. There on purple velvet lurked the murder weapon. Was I to blow myself away on my birthday? Was that the message? And I gingerly extracted his business card from under the black barrel.

No affection. No happy returns. Only his signature plus a strong smell of cigars which, however, did strike me as an intimate note. For Father's very flesh exudes a smell of fine tobacco although he is fanatically opposed to smoking. It's one of his vexing paradoxes that keep you guessing.

Did he come by the smell through osmosis? For tobacco ranks high on the golden scale of his multinational ventures, though at his office and house smoking is strictly verboten. I still recall with a thrill when, home from boarding school at Christmas, I sneaked into the armory and crunched my cigarette into the million dollar visor of a Maximilian soldier as the strains of *Silent Night* floated in from another wing of our baronial mansion.

•

But the gun triggered no such memories from my school days at Hotcock's—a nickname which we perennially horny youngsters had bestowed upon Hitchcock's Academy. I loathed the school. I couldn't wait till the next break, except for fall when my old man was sure to drag me along on another one of his hunting trips in the northern woods and bust my balls, teaching me to shoot for the kill like a man.

I refused. The crown of a deer would emerge from the thicket. He'd whisper, Aim. I'd stare at the ground and fire into the pine needles.

At last he gave up making a man of me. Enough's enough, he muttered through his teeth. He grabbed the rifle from my sweaty hands and strode off in contemptuous silence, his crimson coat fading slowly among the tall, impervious trees.

I stayed behind, for once ahead of the game, and twice relieved as I peed into the carpet of dry needles.

•

His failure to punish me must have gnawed at his ego, and the gift of the gun was the kick in the ass he burned to give me but dared not deliver that day long ago in the woods. Alone in the northern woods with an obstreperous son who was still holding daddy's rifle and maybe wasn't quite the poor shot he pretended.... A farfetched assumption? Perhaps. But a logical one. I saw him pace the length and breadth of his armory in the night, up and down and back and forth, at the front and the rear of his troops, calculating how to get even with me; and crashing with a deafening clatter smack into the bulging breastplate of one supposed Duke of Clone whose hidden blade...

The action stopped and my heart skipped a beat or two as an old wives' tale leaped into my consciousness:

A knife for a gift spells foul luck.

A knife...or a gun? I whispered with a furtive glance at the evidence I'd unwisely placed alongside a yet to be completed work: a nest of three metal rings which had taken on an eerie resemblance to the Duke's neck guard.

He's put the whammy on my project. Now I may never get it done, I thought. And I whisked the gun out of sight to dump with the trash after dark. What if he found out? It sure would tickle his animus if not his anus to know how he can play fast and loose with my superstitions which he lampoons because they happen to be mine.

He, of course, professes to have none. But I doubt it. His brain may well be loaded with totemic curses, their drumbeat thumping through the night as they roll from time immemorial into the now of his sleep.

Ghosts of his youth. I see them glide past his Spartan bed and meld into the shadow walls—a voiceless nocturnal parade in savage prehistoric masks and modern drag.

•

Once upon a time Father was bewitched by the far away past. He would become an archaeologist, would excavate the vestiges of early man and crack the mystery of the Greek *mysterion*. It was to be the fulfillment of a passionate dream.

Why let himself be sucked into business, play patsy to a family tradition, a world completely alien to his nature? If he loses his inheritance, amen. It may be for the best. He'll make his own fortune, start at the bottom and rise to the top. His destiny was written in the stars.

I am paraphrasing from a letter to Mother, whom he began to court while she was still in her early teens and he already a graduate student at university.

My dear little lady, he wrote. I have told you my ultimate dream.

•

A short-lived dream. Did he kill it or merely give it a twist? Trade in one dream for another? Instead of digging for the elusive past, he's opted for its always reliable hardware. He has chosen an outrageously expensive pastime. I don't see how he could indulge in it without the megabucks of corporate business.

So I ruminate while I lie on my bed, killing time to survive the day after. A fat fly crawls up and falls down on the snow-crusted window. And the monotone chant of a crazy or drunk sounds like a sacred mantra as it rises from the Sunday hush of my deserted street.

•

His letters to Mother. For years I'd been burning to get my hands on them. He had declared them off limits and she would not cross his orders. But on that fateful day of the gun, a miracle occurred. She took the letters from the safe, determined to show them to me. I now regret that I didn't ask what triggered her singular act of defiance which was also her last. She died soon after.

You may read them at the house. Your father won't be home till late, she had assured me on the phone. It's your birthday and since you've always been so curious about our courtship, I mean the letters.... I wish the two of you could be friends....

Friends? A sweet wish, but an unlikely option, I thought as I made the pilgrimage to the house, content that the old man wouldn't be lurking inside while I was digging up what he was anxious to withhold from me.

Marching north in a brisk April wind, from downtown to the family stronghold, I pictured him at his club holding court by the fire in a chiaroscuro of aged mahogany and tooled leather, validating a billion dollar deal with a bourbon straight up. One shot was his self-imposed limit.

The scene kindled a whim to join him in a drink by the fire, but was quickly snuffed out as a cabby screeched to a halt at my feet with the prophetic cry, Ahgonnakillallyafuckinmawthafuckers!

So, having skirted death while sleepwalking through Manhattan's worst gridlock, I arrived in front of the house.

There at the royal gate I took a breather. I scraped a mess of dog shit off my shoe. I lit a cigarette and offered one to the security guard, a lad black as the road and fantastically handsome.

Light up, my friend. The man's away.

He looked amused, but he refused. Not at work, sir. The man's away. A reassuring thought. However, gaining the vestibule, I was haunted by the notion that he was still in his castle, checking my every move through the eye holes of a battle-bruised Teutonic suit of armor which stood guard by the staircase to Mother's quarters, a spiral staircase, ripped off some 13th century cloister and smuggled out of Thessalonike to be bought by him for a steal.

He tailed me with the echo of my footsteps as I began the circular ascent, his shadow merging with mine on the ramp up and around the spiral.

•

Hurry, dear!

Mother waving me on from the top of the stairs in a black cloud of chiffons—a gown designed to masquerade her weight. To me she resembles a widow in mourning over a dead marriage.

You look tired, Jamsie. Do you get enough sleep?

I sleep far too much, Mother.

Me too. Sometimes I sleep all day. She smiles. The black cloud floats into the living room. Her boudoir. On a fragile table, amid lacy tea things and bric-a-brac, the box with his letters. A plain, gray metal box. A poor doll's coffin.

Your father needn't learn of our secret. Hush.... Did you hear? She clasps my hand and listens—for the sound of his car? His voice? I have heard nothing.

It was nothing. Don't mind me, Jamsie. I had a bad night.

She takes the letters from the box and sits down below the window facing east: a cathedral window of Art Nouveau stained glass erotica. Anorexic, ivy-crowned unisex nudes cavort among tropical creepers and lilies in mildly suggestive poses which spawned my first adolescent orgy of masturbation on her cushiony couch.

She is handing the letters over to me. Not a word to your father. Promise. And please do read him with charity.

•

With charity for all, oh Mother, still shielding the man for whom you have ceased to exist, except at public functions when he needs you by his side to prove his dubious masculinity with a load of romantic bull, kissing the nape of your neck as he helps you out of your wrap, brushing over your bosom as if by accident, acting the horny hubby. Disgusting.

She sits below the darkening window, faceless, shapeless, useless from long neglect—his little lady, the wisp of a girl he courted for her lively childlike beauty, and married—why? To certify his manhood black on white? Or for her dad's political connections? Or after all for love?

I switch the lights on. Charity? I'll make an effort, Mother.

I help her get up from the low-slung couch. We embrace. And gathering the folds of her black gown, she leaves me alone with his letters.

•

They were held together by an unromantic rubber band which snapped as I riffled the pages, like so many playing cards. Which was the joker? I broke the pack and picked a letter. Would my old man sweep down in vengeance from Mt. Olympus? For the letter gave a graphic account of Hera bathing nude in the sacred spring to recover her virginity after Zeus had invaded her maidenly body.

At first blush I figured he'd used the top god's pubescent wife as a stand-in for Mother—a case of metaphoric child abuse, I told myself. But scanning the text again, I had to scratch that interesting contingency. His dear little lady was wiped off the picture. (As for his identity with Zeus, you be the judge.)

I reexamined the text in search of a clue. He'd hiked and picnicked in the woods with friends. They had hunted for a secluded stream to bathe in the nude at sundown and found it in "a piny grove awash with the sylvan aura of ancient Greece."

So far so good. But the friends—are they female or male? Are they both? He won't say. Like Mother they fall by the wayside as he sails off on his own nonstop from Massachusetts, USA, into a mythical Grecian sunset.

Naked among granite boulders he is watching through the laurel in a gold and copper light. Watching. Waiting. Never touching. Bathing small, pebble-slick breasts with his eyes. Bathing hairless mount veneris pebble sleek between slim boy thighs...

Forgive me if I've paraphrased too freely. It's some months since my birthday, the day of the gun, and my memory, unlike Father's, is not photographic. However,

I can assure you that I have faithfully retained the spirit behind the letter. One has to read my old man between the lines.

•

My dislocation from Mother's cozy boudoir to an arcane Hellenic spring was quickly dampened by a shot from the bottle she had graciously left with the unconsumed birthday cake. Glass in hand, I ambled about the room, skirting costly, poorly balanced lamps and screens and similar unstable items, while from above the fireplace, a pigtailed school girl was staring down at me through marble blue eyes. And below this life size non-portrait of hers, my mother had arranged all sorts of knick-knacks and souvenirs, miniature boxes, family photos, an ornate porcelain clock—and yes, as if by accident, one laurel branch.

•

Mother's place a showcase of bourgeois kitsch? You bet. But I feel at home in her quarters, my only safe retreat in this petrified museum or mausoleum we call our home. However, Father, the famous collector with the infallible eye—how does he feel about the stuff she brought with her from the nouveau riche suburbia of her childhood? You'd expect him to make her adjust to his high standards. She would do anything for him.

But perhaps the schlock turns him on—like some highbrow gents who can only get it up in a lowbrow brothel? An intriguing idea. I chewed on it for a while before I returned to the letters. And there I found an abrupt change in tone. No more pubescent goddesses. No leering Zeus. The sunset glow of Hellas had washed off the canvas and the letters read like a logbook. Maybe they were a substitute for it—detached in tone; a no-nonsense record of daily events, such as athletics in which he excelled. Diving, fencing, shooting and every ball game (but no balling) on or off campus. In short he dwelled on the sporting fame of his alma mater which—you guessed right—is also mine: a hoary, ivy-suffocated neo-gothic cluster of brick where our forebears whet their claws and wits. In sum, a university, heavily endowed by the family and thus beholden to corporate politics.

Now and then his script might veer off the track, and onto the page would vault an impetuous "to hell with statistics!"—implying he had it with economics, his major to accommodate his dad, he insists. Yet he continues as an honor student in the field he despises and denounces as a pseudo-science. And he proudly lists his top grades and each reward, as though he were hoping to impress not his little lady but his big dad.

He also mentions auditing a course or two in anthropology. But I find no hint that he intends to make the study of ancient man a lifetime ambition.

•

Suddenly the unforeseen. The joker in the pack of cards pops up in the shape of L.C.: a splendid looking older man of forty plus. A mental giant. Rhodes scholar & rodeo champ. Expert on jazz & Wagner. Creator of *psychoanthropologic archaeology*, an academic discipline he invented to stump his colleagues. Visiting prof & temp dept chair, his predecessor, a notorious hophead, having dropped dead after ingesting a yet to be analyzed substance from a pre-Columbian two-headed bowl.

I have culled the info from a medley of letters. Since few bear a date—an oddity of which I shall have to say more—it is uncertain just when my old man parlayed himself into the class of a campus legend whose popularity was so immense, one student was trampled to death in a stampede for seats.

According to the *Boston Bugle*, L.C. arrived at the graveside in tears to deliver a heart-rending eulogy. And the fire department issued an order to restrict attendance of L.C.'s classes to twelve.

•

We have no hint why Father missed the deadline for registration. My guess is he overslept. When he tries to register belatedly and is rejected, his rage is boundless. A petty, ignorant bureaucracy has spat on his rights and he will demand a public apology.

Don't those assholes know who I am? Who my family is? He'll lay his grievances before the board of directors and force them to exempt him from the rules, or else.

Dreams of glory. Dreams of gore. Papal dispensation for the crown? If it weren't for dad, I'd switch to Princeton tomorrow.

All this for the eyes of a schoolgirl who couldn't care less. But that won't stop him. His ego, that delicate structure of glass, is cracking, and my future mother is a convenient dumping ground for plots of revenge.

Scratch the board of directors. Take the bull by the horns. Tomorrow he will audit L.C.'s classes, come hell or high water. Then, only then, if he deems the lecture worthy of his time and money, will he demand the professor's OK for belated enrollment.

...a fair request, sir, which you can dignify with a stroke of your facile pen, he states in an imaginary dress rehearsal. *It won't prick my conscience to sit at your feet as your thirteenth disciple. But should it prick yours, a hired gun may be provided at your discretion to sacrifice one of the twelve and thus remain within the confines of the ordinance.*

A jest, my good man. Just a jest. But be on guard. I have other tricks up my sleeve. For I come from a time-honored line of legalized tricksters, tradesmen, clergymen, aldermen, councilmen, congressmen...

Here the pedigree breaks off. The last word is inked out. But as I hold the letter to Mother's rose-shaded lamp, I swear I see the word *hangmen* under the ink.

Perhaps I misread. I can only report what I saw. I saw the gallows.

•

His vengeful ruminations may have propped up his ego and helped his digestion. A guy rejects you and you want to pay him back in kind. It's human nature. It's mine. But Father hasn't met the guy, not yet. He may have spied him from afar on campus, under an umbrella in the rain, or in a distant window through the trees in a whirlwind of autumn leaves. But he had met him on a photo. He was still in boarding school when, browsing in a second hand bookstore, he ran across one of L.C.'s earliest works. A well-thumbed, amply illustrated first edition. The title, *Fertility Rites and Sacrificial Cannibalism among the Murrhians of the Lower South Pacific*, arouses instant curiosity. He buys the book and risks expulsion as he studies the dog-eared pages under the desk at Hitchcock's Academy, another family endowed institution where I too received primal enlightenment with one hand under the desk.

•

Graphic diagrams of sacred rites. Naked dancers male or female dressed in nothing but tattoos. Coiled on coral sand, the Shaman transmorphing into the self-devouring serpent. Uncoils his long lean body, slithers, writhes. Spits in a sudden spray of sea foam and rears, penis in mouth, mouth his vagina.

Oops! Hardporn anthropology causes sex glands to produce too quickly. He is about to shut the book. But as though ordered by a subliminal voice, he turns to the next page and there is the author.

There he sits, the great L.C., crosslegged by the ocean as he worships a phallic rock in a circle of tribal chieftains. Their bodies are tattooed. His is in khakis. And while the black Murrhians faces of his hosts are hidden behind horned, wooden masks, the face of their discoverer is bare, its whiteness sliced in two uneasy halves by the shadow of his tropical helmet.

•

So much for Father's adolescent vagaries. As for his adult schemes of revenge, they weren't only childish, they were unnecessary. If the registrar had shut him out, L.C., a law unto himself, would let him in. He should have approached the professor's lectern and asked for his permission. It was that simple.

In fact, he did precisely that. He made his request at the start of the first session, a bit weak in the knees perhaps, but in control of his emotions and demeanor as behooves a young gentleman of his status or mine. And—abracadabra—he was welcomed into the fold, not as the thirteenth disciple but more likely as the thirty-third.

•

I rub my eyes in disbelief. Father, whom I never saw defer to anyone, defers to L.C. as the master. *Dig up the vestiges of ancient man. Breathe life into the corpse and make it dance.* Chalked on blackboard in exquisite penmanship by the master.

Need I say more? Father, copying the phrase into his notebook, takes pains to match the exquisite penmanship, but happens to write *lice* instead of *life*, a slip of the pen which he confides to the professor during an evening walk by the fogged river. L.C. reacts with wholesome laughter, but counsels due respect for such supposed slips—not for their paronomastic potential, he cautions, but for their cosmic relevance. And he follows up with a long discourse on the symbiotic absolute of life for which the lowly louse is no less fitting an example than is the mighty oak, etcetera etcetera.

Leave the flat land! Climb to the top of the mountain! Spread your wings and follow the eagle's flight beyond good & evil!

Comments Father: The master held me spellbound for nearly an hour. What a brain! What a man! A scholar with a poet's soul. And how he loves to quote Nietzsche!

•

Upon the word Nietzsche I burst into a volley of sneezes. A draft was blowing down my neck and the door slammed shut with a bang like a shotgun blast. Not the sort of blast one would expect in this neighborhood. I opened the door a crack to make sure that the royal fort hadn't come under attack by what's called hereabouts the elements. But the only element was the wind as it howled through the marble vestibule, whistled up the monastic stairs and sent the letters helterskelter through the room.

I crawled on all fours to pick them up while I wondered again why so few had a dateline. A man as time obsessed as my old man—why would he omit the date line? Of course he was a young man at the time, I had to prompt myself. Still I was puzzled.

Granted, a hint as to backdrop or weather helped me paint in the seasons. Autumn announced itself in a purple blaze of falling leaves. They stormed through the letters. They twirled, they rustled and crackled. One spotted maple leaf, fragrant and faultlessly shaped, sailed into my lap, though when I held it to the light, it crumbled to dust.

But most of the time it was winter. The campus was snow bound, and on the frozen pond in the night two silhouettes—L.C. and Father?—were skating under the starlight to a distant radio. *Liebestraum*? But when did the nocturnal shadowplay take place? What month? What day? What hour?

You think I'm making a fuss over nothing. But think again. We aren't dealing with a slob like me who can't tell yesterday from tomorrow. We are dealing with my father, a stickler for punctuality. In his ledger, time is money. He works, eats, plays, sleeps, shits by the clock. He holds himself and all of us to a strict schedule. Not even the dead are excluded.

•

I'll give you a recent example. The night before Mother's funeral, just as I teeter on the edge of sleep, having tossed and turned and groaned in my hairshirt of guilt (the nameless little things I could have done for her and why didn't I escort her to a revival of *Guys and Dolls*, a musical she adored), at five in the morning, just as I am about to catch some shut-eye before the trip to the cemetery, my old man phones to remind me that he expects me at the house at 9:25 a.m.

The cortège leaves for the cemetery at 9:30 sharp. Whoever is not in the library by then will have to manage on his own. Or hers, he adds with a noisy clearing of his throat. Your mother will be laid to rest at noon.

His throat is clogged with sinus congestion or grief.

I trust we won't have too many delays. The TV crew may slow us down, not to speak of those interminable elegies. I've put a cap on length and number. But there's no guarantee. People, especially our politicians, glory to hear their own voice, no matter how moronic the palaver. And God help us if my senile father-in-law should get it into his besotted head to orate nonstop in front of the mausoleum.

A snarl. A heavy cough. Then a sly chuckle. Well, son, I doubt you'll have to suffer through his blarney once they haul my mortal shell to the charnel house.

He does have a streak of humor, however grim. But it would have been no joke if I'd gone to sleep and missed the cortège.

I almost missed it. Not that I fell asleep. I was too distraught. But I wasted precious minutes in futile search of a black tie. I had to borrow one in a hurry—from whom? My best bet was my namesake, the bartender Jimmy. I raced over to Paddy's where more precious minutes went down the drain and drinks down the hatch before generous but shaky Jimmy had secured his clip-on bow tie to my Brooks Brothers shirt.

The motorcade with the family car at the head was already on the move when I got to the house. But the car reserved for the household staff idled long enough for me to squeeze in with the help. They were in tears. They all had loved my Mother.

•

You never know what form my old man's vengeance might take if you fail to be prompt. A few weeks ago I was summoned to his office for 5 p.m. to countersign a document in connection with Mother's will. Anxious to get there as ordered, I left home an hour ahead of time. But a shootout and two false arrests on the subway made me 12 minutes late.

12 piddling minutes. I confirmed the time on the clock in the gloomy foyer. And his secretary wouldn't allow me beyond the reception room.

Your father had to leave for a board meeting, this trouble-shooting, busty matron, another Mrs. Q, proclaimed. Your father waited till the stroke of 5. Then he departed.

Departed, my ass. While the false Mrs. Q was mouthing what the boss had drilled her to say, I swear I heard and smelled him from the far end of the long corridor and even caught a glimpse of him on the phone, wheeling and dealing in a voluminous cloud of cigar smoke which permeates every nook and cranny of this labyrinthian building—one of the oldest and least imposing, one of the most sinister structures in the shady shadow canyons of America's financial heart.

•

Time is money. He meant to teach me the usual lesson, I figure, as I blow my cigarette smoke in concentric circles up to the fat-bellied puttis on Mother's

36

porcelain clock. Tick tock. We have clocks all over
the house. But not in the armory. Down there in the
Stygian silence of the light and temp controlled bun-
ker, time is measured by centuries or millenniums.
Measured. Counted. Approximated or appraised.
Whichever you prefer, one constant remains: Time is
Money. The older the product, the higher the value.
But there's a catch, daddy-o. The older the product,
the less reliable the timing. Which is to say you have
paid more for less.

Not that I'd have the nerve to tell him. Besides,
my brand of logic would rightly appall him.

Don't think with your ass. Use your head!

And he loses himself in a pep talk on the mind-
boggling progress of microelectric hightech in this age
of the holy computer or haloed laser, and how one of
his rarest finds, a Grecian helmet with a chunk of the
warrior's brainpan stuck in the bronze through millenniums, has just been retested and moved at least
two centuries back in time.

We are witnessing momentous quantum leaps. The
latest testing methods are bound to be obsolete in no
time. It won't be long and the counterfeiters will have
to close up shop and go begging.

You notice how my father's faith in the beneficial
progress of science borders on the religious. But not
to worry. Should a glitch occur and an acquisition
prove a fake, he'll either pawn it off to a gullible buyer
or make it a tax-deductible gift to a public museum.
Whichever way, he wins.

•

But please don't call my old man a common cheat. His ethics hardly differ from our politicians'. It's his temperament that makes a difference. On him, intrigue works like a drug. He plays the game the way an addict shoots up. I've often envied him the high he must get from his devious maneuvers. Doesn't he ever crash?

For years he has indulged in a cat & mouse game with the GAA, the Gallery of Arms & Armor. He strikes up a friendship with the curator and gets to borrow his expert maintenance crew three times a year. They show at the bunker to keep the collection in shape; disassemble each single armor, cleanse, lubricate the zillion parts and reassemble them again—a complicated, time-consuming operation which doesn't cost my old man a dime. The service is gratis.

That little curator...says Father. Thinks he's putting one over on me. Butters me up while he keeps track of the obits, sure my collection will go to the GAA. That little East European... Will he be surprised!

The curator is Jewish, Father knows. But presently, in our circles, it isn't kosher to slander the Jews, though we have plenty of other minorities left to slander. Our fluctuating politics inform our social mores. It's like playing Musical Chairs.

•

I'm drafting a new will, he informs Mother over the phone between two board meetings. The collection is to remain in the house which I shall designate as a semi-public museum. Your residential privileges are of course guaranteed for life.

And the GAA? Mother ventures.

They won't be forgotten, dear heart. I'm leaving them my second best Wheellock rifle.

•

The dreaded allure of his armory... The phalanxes of hollow knights who used to pound the walls of my dreams. These days I don't dream much, not in my sleep. But the dread remains. Father will see to that.

Why else would he wax eloquent over the armorers? Sorry, I have no other phrase for his rhetoric. He exalts them as the blessed muse behind the clumsy war machine of yore. I am quoting him verbatim.

Those armorers were artists, my boy. Real artists!

What a travesty. He summons me to the bunker under some flimsy pretext and instantly proceeds to belittle me or my work via the Dark Ages when he's never seen my work, having refused to visit the loft or my shows, save for the last one. And we know how that ended. Besides, he was already blind.

The armorers! Their matchless skill and patient toil in overheated primitive smithies! Blood & sweat but no complaints. Happy, motivated men in dingy dungeons. He hammers away like a union-busting boss until my head's about to split. But do I tell him off? Not me. I tag along like a dog from armor to armor and never open my trap.

He will stop in front of an unspectacular battle suit and proclaim it a masterpiece of technical know-how, unparalleled in modern art—meaning my art, of course. It shows in his body language and provocative asides, like "naturally, you have to know your math." Or "your metals."

Take the dome of this helmet—forged from a single sheet, he lectures me. See for yourself. No seams. Not a trace of welding. And only a minimal difference in the thickness of the steel. That, my boy, is what I call precision work. And he gives me the "I betcha can't do that" look.

Precise calibration! Art! See how he taunts me, first with the dome of the helmet, then with the bulge of the breastplate—another inimitable masterpiece, calibrated to resist the deadliest sword thrust... Damn! There goes the phone. No, wait! Stay where you are!

Where am I? I stare at the breastplate. And while my old man is quoting disembodied figures over the phone, it dawns on me that I am standing face to visor with the battle suit of the Duke of Clone or Cloyn, the same duke whose misplaced codpiece may have prompted my old man to excise the GAA from his will.

•

Father and the codpiece. I can't resist running that farcical interlude for you. It happened on Thanksgiving Day a good many years ago, the final year of my grind at Hitchcock's. My homecoming coincided with Father's. He had just returned bronzed and relaxed from a business trip to Saudi Arabia, and the desert sand was still on his loafers when he asked me to join him on an inspection tour of his troops. While he'd been out of the country, the crew from the GAA had done their seasonal job. A faint smell of their chemicals lingered as we entered the bunker.

Everything looked spit-and-polish. Father had no complaints—until we got to the duke. Something missing down center under the breastplate. He stared into the emptiness between the plated thigh guards and clutched his crotch. What had happened to the codpiece? The vital shield which saved the manly warrior's manhood from being blown straight to hell— where was it? Stolen! But I had already spotted the item which to my instant merriment dangled from the steely thumb of the duke's gauntlet. I burst into laughter and, hitchhiker style, pointed with my thumb.

Stop laughing, you moron. Who is to blame for this vandalism? This insult? This desecration, he added darkly. Can you tell us?

Much as he would have loved to pin the blame on me, he couldn't. I had been in school. So where to look next for a logical suspect if not among the crew from the GAA? Their curator had recently hired some types of dubious complexion, politically and otherwise; malcontents who made it their agenda to defecate on our race and class. They'd had the opportunity. They had a motive. However... Father hesitated. Can we substantiate the charge? We have no proof.

And what, I thought, would be the charge if we had proof? Conspiracy to castrate an armor? I tried to keep a straight face. The crew may have forgotten to put the piece back where it belonged—an oversight, pure and simple, I suggested.

Not bloody likely, he shot back. And snapping his fingers, he sent me upstairs to inform Mother that he'd be ready within twenty minutes to "perform the ritual carving of the bird." That's verbatim what he said, I swear.

So on that sunny Norman Rockwell day of grace and plenty, the GAA got kicked out of the will because of a missing codpiece.

•

Or am I jumping to the wrong conclusions? God moves in mysterious ways. Something tells me the old man never intended to leave his collection to anyone. There could be no separation. Deep down in his heart he must always have known that he and his armors were destined to stay together, even in death.

So my thoughts meander back and forth while Father, much alive, is still on the phone.

A deal's a deal, I hear him say. His voice seems to come from the armor. And I imagine him embalmed inside, eternally welded or wedded to his collection. In touch with business by phone as has been said of Mary Baker Eddy in her coffin.

•

Look, he's back at my side! But he has changed into a different father. Business… He sighs. No peace in my own house. Forgive the awkward interruption, Jimmy.

My old man apologizing—to me? If anything, I ought to apologize to him for having just confined him to his coffin. And he's called me Jimmy. I haven't heard that since I was a little kid.

When I asked you down—OK, I ordered you, if you insist—it wasn't to give you a lecture on the armorer's craft, however worthy a subject… A pause. A dismissive shrug. The gulf between us is shrinking.

I have a surprise for you, Jimmy. It's waiting in front of your nose, right there on the bulge of this breastplate, this functional cuirass. No frills. No ornaments on it—correct? Now watch. Watch closely.

He's pushed up his cuffs and loosened his wrists— a magician performing his ultimate stunt. His hand runs over the breastplate and halts above the spot where the bulge dips to the waist.

What do you see, Jimmy? His voice is down to a whisper.

Not much, dad. Maybe a smudge? A discoloration?

Step closer. But easy. Don't get your breath on it.

He's pulled a magnifying glass from under his frayed Shetland sweater.

Now look through the glass.

I inch forward and hold my breath. The smudge is evolving into an intricate design the size and shape of a penny. Magic?

Mythology in the round! He's drawn a circle in mid-air. He guides my eye in the lens as Noah's Ark comes floating in on hairpin waves. A minuscule ark. A minuscule cargo. Men and women wrapped in shawls. Swaddled infants. Livestock and wild beasts. A living huddle among baskets, barrels and bundles. The dove has spread her wings in flight, an olive twig in her beak.

Look at the olive twig, how it bends with the wind; how the veins are etched into the tiny leaves! Minutiae which the naked eye would miss. Without the magnifier we'd be blind...

He's dimmed the lights and stands stooped and wordless with his hands over his eyes. I thought he'd never speak again but he's already straightened his shoulders.

Well then. I trust the surprise was big enough for you.

God yes. But his sudden reversals are always bound to be the biggest surprise. You'd think by now I ought to be used to the act, that for me his new hat is old hat. Not so. He puts it on and—pronto—he's succeeded in blowing my mind all over again.

•

A microscopic precious etching on an ordinary battle suit—how did it get there, why? Father isn't asking me, and if I had a drop of common sense I'd leave him to himself. But I stay.

Is it a good luck charm? he demands into space. The seal of an underground guild? Or a religious graffiti, done on the sly by some fanatic genius—an outlawed Manichee? A defrocked monk? A Jewish or Islamic mystic? I'm beating my brains out trying to solve the puzzle—what for? For Christ's sake. WHY?

His outcry echoed through the bunker. He was looking me straight in the eye and I looked away, embarrassed as though he'd caught me watching him masturbate or stealing pennies.

Get out of here! I warned myself. I'll scream if I don't leave this minute. But I stayed and even made a feeble attempt to cheer him up.

If you can't solve the puzzle, dad, who can? Your armor is much too unique.

Much too unique? He smiled indulgently. Sufficiently unique to make it priceless in terms of money. But I didn't buy it as an investment. Come, let me explain.

He took my arm. And walking me to the exit, he gave me the story. For him it was an unusual story, since he had bought the armor on blind faith. It happened on a business trip in London when he was approached by a dealer who claimed descendance from the ducal line of Cloyn or Clone. The armor, he claimed, was an heirloom.

Perhaps it was an heirloom. Father chuckled. No ducal house of Cloyn or Clone existed. The dealer was a fake. But the armor was no fake! It was authentic mid fifteenth-century English, the workmanship impeccable though not rare for that period. He was on the verge of declining the offer when he noticed the scratches. They ran in such a perfect circle he couldn't pass them off as a fault in the metal.

(So the purchase wasn't altogether blind...) You got yourself a bargain, dad?

We agreed on a fair price, rejoined daddy the cagey collector, adding with disarming frankness that he would have bought at any price. He was ready to spend a fortune.

Call it what you will—delusion? I had to own the almost invisible image, the hidden myth within the smallest circle, the Greek Mysterion...

Here Father caught himself and abruptly changed gears. Big words. They tell us nothing. More likely than not I fell for an old boyhood dream, the quest for the hidden treasure. Well then. Back to the boardroom. I'm glad we talked, Jimmy.

I'd have loved to throw my arms around him. But we only shook hands. And on that civil note we split as he waved me through the electronic eye of the exit.

•

A happy ending in the bunker? Don't be fooled. Such endings are an exception. As a rule we end up where we started—I the whipping boy, he the whip. He might draw my attention to a fancy parade suit that's choked in ornaments from spiffy casque to swanky boots, and you can bet your bottom dollar I'm in for another beating—on teamwork this time around.

Not that he favors the baroque. But it makes for a handy model to demonstrate the virtues of teamwork: welders and goldsmiths, historians, engravers and sculptors, ballistic experts—Artists! He stares at me to let that brick sink in. Oh yes my boy! Those chaps did not create in splendid isolation, pampering their ego, contemplating their navel! They wouldn't have lasted. The public would have made short shrift, stripped them, hauled them naked as a jaybird to the commons, broken them on the wheel, flogged them to death...

Father's face turned cherry red. His litany of torture had gotten out of hand. He tore at his necktie. He teetered and clasped his heart—about to drop dead? But no. He slowly pulled himself upright, and breathing deeply, he covered the length of the bunker with measured steps.

When he faced me again, his color was back to normal, a bronze, well preserved suntan. In short, he said calmly as though nothing special had occurred, ideally speaking, an armor should be battleproof as well as aesthetically pleasing. You understand?

I guess I do. I guess it's a matter of taste, your galloping into the bloody slaughter fest aesthetically dressed in 300 lbs. of steel. An elaborate form of torture? But watch yourself, dad.

•

There was that night when Mother came home late from one of my more festive openings, giddy with champagne and fun. Father met her in the empty vestibule. His reception for the Shah of Iran had ended hours ago. Her presence had been expected. What had kept her?

So far so good. He was irritated but not angry and she could have got off with a fib—a class reunion, a charity meeting, anything except the truth. But her head was in the clouds. She reverted to her former self, the carefree schoolgirl who had caught his fancy at a party. She tossed off furs and shoes and, humming, reached into her oversized tote for the little sculpture she had bought at my show.

Isn't it lovely? It reminds me of a ship. A happy ship. James says that's all right with him as long as it makes me happy. Does it make you happy, darling?

His stone-faced silence should have warned her. But she couldn't let go.

Remember daddy's yacht, the Mary-Jane? He planned it as a wedding gift. But you wouldn't accept it. You said you needed nothing, only me. It made me feel so proud. You were so grand. Remember?

A pleading look, but no response. She ought to have stopped but she couldn't let go and, really, how could she forget the night of their secret tryst on the Mary-Jane, a tall ship moored in Sheepshead Bay and christened after her late mother? How could she forget their necking aboard to the ruckus in nearby waters, the ackackack of machine gun fire connected, perhaps, with one of her daddy's far-flung enterprises?

Prohibition. But no moonshine. Not on the Mary-Jane. She aches to feel him inside. She begs him to take her, though he already said no, absolutely not, no intercourse, not till we're married. Not until my little lady is of age. While his mouth and fingers are all over her body. Her blouse is torn. Her panties are in shreds. But she is still a virgin. That's what counts. The vestibule was cold as ice. Oh love, what do you remember? She sobbed and buried her face in his old sweater.

•

So he sent you flying across the hall. Or did he smash his fist into your face? Come now. It wouldn't be the first time, Mother!

You're wrong. It was an accident. I slipped and fell. At my hairdresser's.

Not at home? On bone dry marble?

Why should I lie? Her bruised face turns away from me.

Don't let him hassle you, ma'am. The maid appears with a new supply of ice. She bends over Mother's bed and fluffs out the pillows. Now you lean back and rest your nerves.

She's tip-toed off. I close the louvered shutters and sit down at the foot of the four-poster bed. Mother's copper hair is striped with shadows. She has fallen asleep.

•

Switch off the gloom of yesteryear and run the tape back to the never-ever land of childhood. I'm sliding down the marble ramp in my fire engine red pajamas and unannounced burst into Father's sacred library. Yes, unbelievable but true, we then were pals.

He's at his desk amid walls of books enshrined behind glass. He's in the same old sweater he wore in college. The early morning sun is dancing on the faded wool, and I see his reflection before I see him.

Hi, dad!

What is it, Jimmy?

It's Sunday, dad.

So my calendar informs me.

But it's my birthday, daddy. I'm five!

Hurrah! He's on his feet and lifts me into the air higher and higher until my head is in the chandelier. A thousand crystal prisms jiggle and jingle. My daddy wears a rainbow in his hair. He lowers me and swings me around five times. Brushes the sleep tangled hair off my eyes and honors me with a kiss on the forehead. Many happy returns, old man!

How many, dad? A billion?

That's mighty steep, Jimbo!

He's swivelled the desk chair up as high as it goes. Piles the Encyclopedia Britannica on it and me on top of the pile. We face each other man to man across his enormous desk. I am taller than my tall daddy.

Well then. Let's talk turkey, pardner.

He picks a pencil from the jaws of a Chinese dragon and leans back in the visitor's chair. When I had my fifth birthday, he recalls, your grandfather gave me a tour through the stock exchange.

I ask was it fun, and he says it was noisy. Yelling traders, ringing bells. He can't recall much else.

When you were two—remember Jimmy?—you used to sing the ABCs for me...

His gray flecked eyes are swimming into mine. His voice—a thin falsetto—comes from behind glassed-in books.

now I know my abc's
tell me what you think of me

I think it's kidstuff, daddy!
Kidstuff. Right on the button!
He shushes a fly off his forehead. He sharpens the pencil. Well then. As of today we are older and smarter. Smart enough to advance beyond fundamentals.
He shuts one eye, takes aim and shoots the yellow pencil precisely into the scarlet jaws of the dragon.
I'm talking armor, James. The ABCs of armor. That's what we must study next.
The what? I'm apprehensive but curious. I don't understand, dad.
You will. Carthage wasn't sacked in a day.
He gets up and says a few words to the gardener under the window, then sits again. But this time he is sitting high above me on top of the desk.
You've been privileged to see more armor than most little boys your age. But did you ever ask yourself what they are made of? No, not the little boys! The armor. We don't think they're made of puppy dog tails—do we now!
No, siree!
Well then. Let's learn what they're made of. We'll start this coming Sunday. I'll meet you in your room after church. If you learn fast—and I see no reason why you won't—you shall be rewarded. A reward after each lesson. How does that strike you, Jimbo?
Wow! I'm so excited I fall off my perch, the encyclopedias tumbling behind me as my bottom hits the floor. No plushy rugs in daddy's library.

No broken bones, I trust? He's pulled me up.

Why not start classes this coming Sunday? I can meet you in your room after church. Agreed, pardner?

Agreed!

A manly handshake sealed the deal. And so began my preschool training under his tutelage. It was a goofy period in my life, excruciating but of short duration. And the fun time that went with the reward was worth every bit of pain.

•

Fun time didn't start right away. There were delays: the lesson itself, for one. Which was further delayed by Nanny who'd stay in my room, in defiance of his order to be out when he came in.

She'd putter about on short, swollen legs, her old face crinklier than ever beneath a fringe of snow white marcelled hair.

Out! he'd command. She wouldn't budge. Arms akimbo she'd glare at him through her wrinkles, ready to spit in his eye. He never looked her in the face—because she had second sight? She used to be Mother's nanny and was still looking in on her from time to time—just in case..., she'd murmur, her pale blue eyes gazing beyond the veil.

Out! He pulled a scroll from under his sweater and brandished it like a sword. Out with you! Or must I carry you out?

No need for that. I still got legs. She hobbled to the door. If you need me, Jimmy, I'll be in my room...just in case... She'd leave the door open behind her. He slammed it shut. Every lesson started with a bang.

Well then. A giant in play-land, he hitched up his pants and cautiously lowered himself onto my toy chest. Squeezed his long legs through the kneehole of my dwarfish desk and unrolled the scroll. Your work chart, he explained. Your primer. I got it finished last night. Meant to have it done before, but business interfered. Too many mergers in one week. Too many boardroom shenanigans. But here they are—the basic parts of the common armor...

The chart rolled back. And helping him flatten it out, I glimpsed what looked like a dismembered robot. Today his drawings, done in pen & ink with eerie technical precision, bring to mind cartoons from Zap or, more disturbingly, a surgical supply store with a display of prosthetic limbs.

His fingers, pliant like a surgeon's, were flicking over the chart. He'd point at one segment. He'd say its name. Then I was to follow up with the same procedure: pointing and naming. Pointing and naming.

No sweat, I said in my innocence.

Well then. Some terms may be unfamiliar. But like the ABC's, they can be memorized. Just look and listen.

I tried. I tried so hard, he lost me completely. And I still can't fathom why a superior brain like my old man's would concoct such insane methodology or what demon prodded him to stuff a gullible five year old with obtuse and useless intelligence.

Of course at the time my dad could do no wrong. But the going was rough and only the promised reward kept me from faking stomach cramps and screaming for mercy. I considered it. But I clenched my teeth and endured. I squirmed and sweated, desperate to follow the terminology as it clonked past my ears and bounced off my skull in a smell of cigars and after-shave lotion. I stammered and stuttered. I splattered the odious chart with my spittle. I was a disaster.

However, this much must be said for my old man: no matter how wretched my performance, he never withheld the reward.

•

By no means perfect. But at least we tried.

He has untangled his legs from under the little boy desk. Grunts. Stretches. Rubs his lower back and moves to nanny's comfortable wing chair. Well then, my lad. He loosens his belt and jiggles his knee. Are we ready to mount our noble stallion?

Am I ready! At the bat of a lash I've straddled his thigh. Giddy up! And off I trot to the leisurely beat of his call—zucchetta, buffeta, tartsche, jamboys and similar gobbledegook which, I discovered later, was no gobbledegook but an alternate glossary for the armor parts he'd forcefed me during the past hour. And that jamboys weren't little boys smeared with strawberry jam, but battleproof miniskirts sported by the manliest of warriors.

Faster! I crack the whip over my stallion's cropped mane and he breaks into a gallop so wild I can barely hang on to his neck as we race through the prairie grass, his snorts louder and faster.

> zuck
>> buff
>>> jam
>>>> bo
>>>>> tart
>>>>>> ta

ra

ta

ta

ha

ah

pff

A last snort in the dried out grass. Then nothing. My dad sits spent and silent in nanny's chair as I let myself roll off his knee and onto the floor. I roll over and over. My head is a balloon. I'm ticklish. I can't stop laughing.

Please, daddy! Play it again!

He never refused.

•

Mother shunned the armory. It was colder than her marriage bed or the grave and she had been the first to call it his bunker. His bunker gave her bad dreams, she'd say when he was out of earshot. But he knew. And yet, incredibly, it was in the armory where he chose to hold her memorial. When I saw his formal invitation in the mail, I tore it up. I would not go. Never.

However, upon further deliberation—my old man's wrath should I decline—I went and even risked jaywalking through lethal traffic to be on time. A needless risk. When I arrived ahead of time, the gates were standing wide open. And entering dreamlike, I found myself whisked to a space where time had ceased to exist.

I was in a timeless garden. Mother's beloved stargazer lilies blazed forth under verdant trees, their sexy perfume tickling my libido. And it took me some gazing and staring before I convinced myself that I was indeed in one wing of the armory and that the rest had been screened off by cascades of willow trees whose fluttery foliage revealed like a quick tease the merest glimpse of naked steel.

Wherever I turned, I found that spirit of fun and romance she had missed as his wife; dainties laid out on the sumptuous buffet in heart-shaped patterns amid white satin streamers and maiden hair; the band tuning up for her favorite music below a canopy of purple orchids; and atop the rococo fountain, a fat little cupid ejecting upon the push of his belly button a golden flow of champagne. It was as though she'd orchestrated her own wake. And the guests were swept off their feet.

They came crowding into her garden, an unlikely bunch of old and new or laundered money no host in his right mind would throw together—except at an Agatha Christie-type weekend or wake. But Mother's witchery blew their disparities into the winds. They tossed off bias and decorum. A West Point general in full regalia had already tossed off his dress coat and fallen into the arms of a Mafia widow.

I'll be seeing you... Mother's song was floating through the oleander, and her garden was swinging and jumping with dance. Her father, older than the hills, leaned ruddy and bemused by the bubbly fountain, a pin with the American flag gleaming from his lapel.

But where was my father, the choreographer of the extravaganza? Where was our host? I searched but I could not find him. Not in the swinging crowd, not in the quiet wings behind the armor. Was he gone forever?

I beg your pardon, sir!

Franz in camouflage fatigues had popped up backstage to report that the chief was engaged elsewhere. He has appointed you his second in command, sir! he concluded military style, though he failed to salute me.

No further info could be wheedled out of him. And to this day I'm at a loss. Why had my old man stayed away?

None of your damned business, I heard myself snarl in his voice. Get cracking, Buster!

I squared my shoulders. I buttoned my coat. I saluted the nearest armor and followed orders. To tell the truth, I had a ball playing my father's double. It seems the role comes all too natural to me.

•

But back to the letters which the storm had blown willy-nilly through Mother's crowded boudoir. Indeed one letter had strayed into the gaping jaws of Father's proudest hunting trophy: the magnificent pelt of a polar bear he had slain above the Arctic Circle during his honeymoon and shipped home to Mother.

A consolation prize for the lonely child bride? I stared into the bear's jaws. The letter was stuck between sharp pointed fangs. And although I was careful to extract it in one piece, it came out badly mauled. Only one line was legible. However one line was enough.

L.C. off on lecture tour. Asked me to sit with his cats. Am deeply honored. Deeply honored to sit with teacher's cats? If that isn't the limit! Has he developed a father fixation on the professor to adopt dream surgeon doublespeak? Don't fret. I'm neither equipped nor inclined to lay my old man on the couch and do a post mortem on his expired soul. The soul that Eros kissed died when he bartered his dream. He'll argue that he bartered nothing, that he only honored his father's wishes. But the defense won't hold, not in my court. His father wasn't a tyrant like mine. And besides, he had a younger son who was scheming in the wings to wear the crown. I can't imagine he'd have killed for it. But you can't tell. He was a potential rival.

So when my old man ascended the throne, he dispatched his kid brother on a humanitarian mission to Guatemala. There he disappeared without a trace—victim of the peasant uprising, the *Times* reported alongside his picture.

A wholesome, clever looking chap. But not clever enough. You can see him broadly smiling from the walls at one of our downtown offices.

•

L.C. descending upon the arena and Father communicates less with his little lady. The letters grow shorter. He doesn't date them. Time is forgotten. Has he fallen in love?

Perhaps not right away. Perhaps at the start it's a crush, the kind I had on my art instructor at Hitchcock's. An urge to be noticed. To force his attention. But before long he is forcing yours. Why else would you see, hear, smell, feel him wherever you are—in a park, on the bus, in the lavatory, at the movies? You know damn well that he has gone to an undisclosed place in the mountains. But mightn't he have stolen into town for a rerun of *Casablanca?* The house is full. The lights go out. The screen has come to life. And there above the shadow sea of heads emerges your hero who squeezes himself into the last remaining seat which, fate has willed, is next to yours. Your thighs have touched. Your head is swimming. Bogie and Bergman dissolve in smoke. Trembling, you turn your eyes and—holy shit! You're rubbing up against the Episcopal bishop's aged mother.

A kiss is just a kiss... The song mocks your wounded heart as you flee from the packed house and through the black night, back to bleak Hitchcock's.

•

Play it again, Sam. Confusion born of desire. What happened to me can happen to anyone. It could have happened to Father. I browse through the letters and the tune of the star-crossed lovers resonates across the campus in the snow.

The heavy snowfall never seemed to end that winter. The scraping of shovels was heard through the night as the great L.C. took charge to help the maintenance staff clear a path to his lecture hall. And though his anti-union activities were the talk on campus and off, the underpaid staff was willing to work overtime for nothing because the professor was a "regular guy." He had them snowed as he snowed my old man who didn't hesitate to leave his warm bed and join the shovel brigade. He doesn't mention it. One has to guess.

One has to decode what he doesn't disclose. He's always played his cards close to the chest. I'm amazed the CIA failed to recruit him. Or am I wrong? Was he or is he still one of their gray moles?

•

Play it again. L.C., Sam in white face, plucking at Father's heartstrings; playing the blues or reading from T.S.E.'s *Waste Land* at the Titanic, a popular old-fashioned off-campus hangout named prior to the maritime disaster, I assume. He might show past midnight to join in a jam session. Or he'd drop by briefly in the afternoon to zoom prestissimo twice through *The Erlking*. His pyrotechnics on the keyboard, he claims, keep his brain from exploding during a scheduled lecture on ritual filicide.

And Father, no music aficionado, hails L.C.'s pianistic wizardry as second to none. It never ceases to astonish me how love plays fast and loose with common sense.

•

Father taking care of L.C.'s cats—what a giveaway, I say as I shuffle the letters. He never allowed a cat into his house. When I sneaked a stray Manx home from Hitchcock's, he had her transferred to the animal shelter. Get her out of my house! At once, Franz!

As usual, I complained to Mother and as usual she pleaded his case: Believe me, it's nothing personal, Jamsie! It's just that your father is allergic to cat hair.

Maybe he is. But that doesn't stop him from feeling "deeply honored" to sit with L.C.'s cats. The phrase in the mauled letter sets the scene. Two sleek felines or a dozen, with myth related names like Amaterasu or Susanowo, hopping onto his shoulder or into his lap, tugging at his knickers in a plaintive symphony of caterwauls, and he kicking them off with a guilt-stricken glance at one of L.C.'s countless portraits. Whichever way he turns, he meets the master's flashing eye—on paintings, graphics, photos, clippings; on busts in bronze and terra cotta. And always in his mind.

Forgive me, he murmurs, communicating with the master in absentia, eyes brimming with tears brought on by cat hair or desire as he relives their walk by the river in the autumnal wind.

•

Did they walk close? Or simply side by side, the way I walked with my art instructor through the fields in the young spring? A thoughtful, quiet man. He taught me the art of looking long and hard at the small things—a leaf, a pebble.

We sat among the buttercups and traced the minutiae of one corona. There was no end to my discoveries. A wealth of design evolved from a petal. A system of form from a stone.

Two bullies from class sneaked out from under a cow hedge. They whistled at us and ran. That night they forced themselves into my room, locked the door, shined a flashlight into my eyes and wrestled me to the floor. One boy sat on my face. The other smeared my dick with paint and wrote *fairytail sweetheart* across my belly.

•

I didn't report them. Snitching could get you killed. At Hitchcock's that was a foregone conclusion. Besides, I was tongue-tied with shame—why? Nothing had "happened" between me and my teacher, much to my lasting sorrow, I should add.

In less than a week he was asked to resign. The school had learned that he shared a studio in town with another artist, and Hitchcock's corridors began to stink with vicious gossip. I had briefly met my teacher's friend—a laid back, older guy, quite old in my young eyes as he answered the door to lend me a book I'd come to borrow.

A rare volume on Etruscan sculpture. It is still among my books. I tried to return it. I rang his bell in spite of the FOR RENT sign in the transom. I rang and rang. I hollered and beat my fists to the door. I sat on the stairs and cried.

No one answered.

•

I sympathize with my old man—up to a point. He alone has been entrusted with the master's keys and cats—a prelude to a love relationship? A ship of love?

Teary-eyed, he sits with the cavorting cats, wheezing, sneezing, yet longing to stay in the house till the end of time; ready to relinquish a fortune, cut family ties and live the wayward life of a "licensed tomb robber"—a term he coined a lifetime later, of course. L.C.'s train is due this afternoon. Father bought out the only florist in town and has filled the house with flowers up to the attic.

A train whistles beyond distant fields and he jumps up to check his watch against the grandfather clock. Too early. He walks about the place, straightening a chair, fluffing a pillow. He transfers three stems of purple orchids from a highball glass to a Japanese vase and back to the glass. He looks out the window. The snow is melting in the yard. An icicle breaks off the porch roof and lands in the cat's dish. He locks the cats in and opens doors and windows to a premature spring. Slowly the pendulum swings back and forth. He counts the minutes.

At last he hears a cab crunch to a halt and he flies to greet the beloved, then stops dead in the slush. A lady with a speckled feather in her hat climbs from the cab and waves with a rolled-up umbrella.

Hello, I'm the missus, he hears her call with a folksy inflection. And you—you must be one of his A-plus students? The one who's looking after our cats?

He nods like a zombie, glued to one spot in the slush while the lady reports that her husband won't be back for at least another week. He is delayed—she forgot by what ribbon cutting duty or other ceremonial activity. He bites off more than he can chew. You know how he is, the dear, wonderful man.

And this, she continues, pointing her umbrella toward a girl who is emerging from a tumble of luggage, this is our Lucy. Back from Quebec after a year at the Ecole Normale. Once she's over her beastly cold, you may like to show her around campus.

Enchanté. He bows stiffly and shakes the mitten of a teenager whose face, as it peels itself from an oversized muffler, bears an uncanny likeness to her begetter's. While from the house, the wife's voice jingles bright and gay in the false spring: Hurry, Lucy! Hurry and look at these heavenly flowers! Your darling daddy! He must have spent a fortune to welcome us home.

•

We'll never know what hit him the hardest, the shock of the unexpected or its awful banality. But a short note reflects the enormity of his hurt.

Am dropping archaeology & related subjects. Shall focus on economy & law. Be sure to give dad the good news when you come to the house Sunday. Tell him I've learned my lesson: Our kind wasn't cut out to survive in a fool's paradise.

•

A fool's paradise—where else does he think we could have survived? I reflected when my old man's voice echoed from another wing of the house. Panicky, I stuffed the letters into the metal box. But much though I pressed and stomped on the lid, it sprang open and the letters spilled over the edges as though his youth had never died and was kicking in its coffin. With a curse I booted the box under Mother's couch and nearly fell down the stairs as I fled from the house.

•

I sit up on my bed and take stock. My body feels rested. The memory junket, interlaced with snatches of sleep, was an effective hangover cure, and last night's binge at Paddy's now seems like a roll of smudged film shot of somebody else's jollifications. But Father's sneak attack at the gallery looms more sinister than before. And bang, the birthday gun is back in focus.

What did I do with it? Where did I hide it? I know I didn't throw it away with the trash outside the building, fearful I'd be observed and implicated in the rape and murder of a prostitute in my precinct.

Paranoid? You're damn right I am. No wonder, what with Father's agents on my tail day and night. I embark on the most time-consuming detours to mislead them. Last week for instance, on my way to an anti-war demonstration in Union Sq., I ferried across the Hudson and back to link up with the marchers in Foley Sq., confident I'd given his men the slip; the phone rings the following morning and my old man announces that he is changing his will.

Think about it, my boy.

No reason given. He's hung up.

You notice how my life in the city has become a game of hide and seek, a losing game since he knows more than I do of my comings and goings. Still, one has to take precautions. Even at home in my loft I routinely search behind the curtain of my makeshift closet while my lover waits down in the hall till it's safe to come up.

And yet—in spite of all the hassle there's a silver lining. For as I rarely have the honor to meet my old man in the flesh, and then by appointment only, his private eyes provide at least a semblance of intimacy.

•

But the gun! All at once its whereabouts are of the utmost urgency and I start on a frantic search. I forage through shelves, drawers, cupboards. I go through my tools. I empty the refrigerator and dip into the toilet tank—a popular stash place in thrillers. I tear through my dirty laundry. I frisk myself. I feel through the pockets of the funeral suit I wore for last night's dismal opening. It lies in a heap on the bathroom floor, wrinkled and filthy, with enough Rorschach type test stains to make me wonder what the hell I was up to when I got myself bombed out at Paddy's friendly neighborhood Bar & Grill.

The loft is a shambles. I give up and sit down on the bed when it dawns on me that I forgot to search the bed.

I lift the mattress. There she lies. For months I've slept, lazed, loved or dreamed with Father's pistol for a silent bedmate.

•

I contemplate her from above as she rests on the faded boxspring—a black solid form, with the crescent moon of the trigger in the trigger guard like a comical afterthought. The gun has evolved into an artifact, detached from its intended function. Unrelated to Father.

The random moon of the trigger, the ruptured logic of the solid form, suggest possibilities. I fetch charcoal and paper and make some sketches. A few more months, and I'll be on Clone and can start work on a new piece. I envisage an oxidized copper assemblage the size of the gun, the symmetry of slanting planes broken by the playful lunar trigger.

•

The phone rang several times. I ignored it and kept sketching until dark. By then the loft was bitter cold. The temperature must have dropped below zero.

I wrapped myself in a blanket and leaned out the window into the atomized snow. Paddy's coach lamp at the corner was a pendulous blur in the night. I felt homesick for Paddy's. Not that I needed a drink. The screaming mimies as Mother might have dubbed the aftermath of last night's binge were gone. I thirsted for the cozy warmth at Paddy's, the boozy talk of old chums down the long mahogany bar, faces aswim in the aged mirror, feet planted in sawdust; and from the urine soaked cubbyhole of a toilet...

Here a bulb lit up in my head. Eureka! I hollered into the winter night. At last I had hit on a safe and appropriate resting place for Father's gun: the rusted tank high up above Paddy's triangular old-fashioned pull-chain toilet.

•

I'm bundled in my storm coat, with the gun tucked inside when the phone begins to ring again. Let it ring till hell freezes over. I'm out of here.

I nearly break the key, double locking my defective door lock. Am halfway down the murky stairs and still hear the phone. An emergency concerning Father? Troubled, guilty and disgusted, I retrace my steps, the ring increasingly demanding as I repeat the rigmarole of lock and key. But the moment I'm in my loft the ringing stops.

Anybody might have tried to reach me, I agree. But I strongly suspect my old man setting up Mrs. Q for one of his nastier tricks. It's happened before, Mrs. Q breathless over the phone, Dear God, your papa...and he cutting in on the armory phone with a sarcastic laugh: Don't set your hopes too high, my boy. My will is signed and sealed. But I am not on my deathbed; a hint that he pictures me on my ass, waiting for him to die. And that I will be on my deathbed, still waiting.

He's right as far as it goes. I am forever waiting, but not for his death. In his perverted mind of course he sees me hunkered down to an enormous breakfast of fried eggs and greasy bacon and homefries and buttered muffins and pots of jam, with both TV or radio blaring so I won't miss a newsbite of his demise.

He's wrong on two accounts. I never watch or listen while I eat. I won't have my appetite spoiled by hemorrhoid commercials and talking heads whose style offends my father's ears while his corporations fatten their purse.

Lastly, I've never yet equated death with bequest. The nouns don't rhyme, not in my little book of dreary verse, though should he check out for good, I won't turn my nose up at whatever he chooses to leave me which is bound to be less than nothing. He probably cut me off decades ago when I balked at shooting like a man in the haunted Northern woods.

But regarding my eating habits, he's on the right track. My diet may shove me ahead of him into the family vault. Even my dealer who couldn't care less whether I'm alive or dead, suggests that I pick something light when I take her to lunch. But I go for vittles that stick to the ribs. And it shows.

Ah yes, your golden boy got middle-aged and fat around the middle. I look in the mirror and can scarcely believe it's me. Whereas Father...

Hasn't gained an ounce since college days. Leaps naked from his Spartan bed at dawn and works out in his hightech gym. Lifts weights. Jumps rope. Shadow boxes. Jogs on a treadmill past a lost dream; breaks sweat as he rows his rowing machine to the virgin goddess' nebulous spring before he dives into his swimming pool and finishes his 60 laps.

Does he still fence, now that his eyes are gone? Don't ever exclude the impossible, not with my father.

I zip my storm coat and don the cap I found on Clone. It swept at my feet with the evening tide on a barnacled log. Did it belong to a young fisherman? The lucky one who lived through Clone's worst hurricane? The cap is my lucky cap.

I pull down the earflaps, pat the inner pocket with the gun for double luck and am off.

•

Behold your antihero rigged out for winter wonderland, upbeat, ready for action. The sudden thrust of frigid air was a shot in the arm. And the latent image—blind naked old man thrusting medieval sword

at armored figment in New World microtech gym—
infused me with an extra dose of vigor. I felt brave
and out of sync like any medieval knight as I sur-
veyed my street which a busted fire hydrant had trans-
formed into a frozen stream.

Did my old man still fish in the frozen wilds, with
Franz the Faithful guiding the rod for him? The question tiptoed through my heart as I tested the ice and
promptly fell on my ass. But in no time I was helped
up by a stranger who had materialized out of thin air
and quick as a flash disappeared into Paddy's saloon,
confirming my hunch that he was one of Father's private agents, prescient of my next move and hungry
for me to make it to nourish his professional ego.

I fooled him, I made my move, but not into Paddy's.
I headed in the opposite direction, northward, ho; up
the middle of the avenue where the traffic, however
sparse, had softened the snow.

The merest sliver of a moon was rising above St.
Patrick's. But the snow shone with its own mysterious
light. The stars were brighter than on Clone, and the
thought that the brightest might be NASA launched
comfort stations in outer space did not dampen my
spirits as I stomped through the bracing cold, alternat-
ing between sidewalk and street while my goggles
steamed over until the whole blessed sky was one
nebula.

I stopped to wipe the lenses when Father's hearse
or a reasonable replica pulled up alongside me and
the driver, hatchet faced like Franz, lowered his window. Hop in, warm up, he lulled through a puff of
vaporized gin. Be our guest, Sonny.

Whatever else he may have lulled was drowned
by the howl of a passing patrol car in whose red-gold
flicker I spied at the limo's rear a U.N. license plate,

and in the upholstered privacy of the interior three clean-shaven gentlemen in tuxedos, with a half nude woman in crotch-high boots stretched motionless across their thighs like a voluptuous corpse.

So that's how our ambassadors to peace spend their off-duty hours and our money—too zonked out to draw the shades, I judged with righteous indignation; while Sonny, tempted to join the party, was stealing another glance.

But Yankee common sense warned to move on. I hadn't lost my head, not quite, not yet. Besides the United Nations was traveling the wrong way.

•

I was steadily advancing north—to storm the ancestral fortress? Drop on my knees before the king and plead his mercy? An odd conceit, yet rational enough if you consider that the bunker used to be my second nursery. For when I was a babe in arms, I was the apple of my father's eye as Mother phrased it, his first and last born man child, safely nestled at his bosom as he carried me about among his armors and fed me tales of self-destructing knights. Such pages from our tenderest years preserve themselves like palimpsests deep in our memory cave, especially if you were born under the no-nonsense star of corporate business.

I had to have it out with him. Let me put it that way. Our clash at the gallery had left me hanging. But believe me, I had not planned on a confrontation, not for this night. You'd no more crash in on his house than you would on the White House. Even an oddball like me won't take that kind of risk.

I proceeded blindly north along the park where, eons ago, I used to make snow angels. The park had frozen into a landscape of glass and in its vast stillness I heard a tree branch crack and break with the sound of shattering crystal.

Behind my back, a stone's throw away, was the house.

•

A stage set of undefined shape, speckled with oscillating lights. That's how I saw my father's house in the frost as I waited in acute discomfort by the bus stop. I had to piss but didn't dare, not here, not in my old man's face, so to speak.

Should I cross the street and avail myself of his facilities in the garage? I wondered, when the bus arrived, discharging toxic loads of carbon monoxide and a person with a monkey on a leash: two fuzzy, sexless city apparitions whom the night had quickly erased. The bus took off without me. And sighing with relief, I pissed into the snow.

A non-event, worth mentioning however since it coincided with a sudden resolve to force myself on him this very night and have it out between the two of us, no matter what.

•

His sidewalk thoroughly de-iced. Scant chance to sue him for a coupla million. I guardedly advance toward the gate, then stand stock still, exposed in a pool of floodlights. Beyond the gate, the Snow Queen's palace has emerged in many-layered splendor and Father's Franz shoots up from behind a shivering mulberry bush.

Hi! Heil! Me thought I glimpsed thee chauffeuring a U.N. limo...

Am pricked by juvenile compulsion to greet him thus, but refrain. He bears no resemblance to what I bumped into a while ago in the night. Distorted vision. Or a midwinternight's dream? The dream goes on. I squint against the glare and ask his permission to enter.

Sir? He's puzzled. Never had orders to keep me out, I conclude as I try to read his face. A curiously boyish face, considering he served in the German Wehrmacht. Must have been one of those countless deluded kids who hurled themselves into the battle for Führer, God and Berlin. A children's crusade. I put a sympathetic arm around the survivor. That, decidedly, was a mistake.

He jerks away and clicks his heels. Shall we go in, sir? We'll have to enter through the back. The alarm system in the front is on the blink again. Shoddy workmanship, says Franz. Poor engineering. This way, sir.

As if I didn't know my way. I always preferred the service entrance when I had the misfortune to reside in my father's house.

•

No, my impatient listeners and comrades, the old man wasn't in. Nor was he dead, unless the corporate jet he had boarded that morning was shot down by a UFO or other militants of uncertain stripe. Franz, who drove him to the tarmac, had returned in time to grant me access. The newly hired security guard may be unfamiliar with my credentials.

So far I've kept my mouth shut. Now, as we march into the kitchen, I ask: whereto was Father flying?

South to a location he, Franz, is not at liberty to name.

OK. I'll ask Mrs. Q.

Mrs. Q! He spits it out like a rotten tooth. The chief decided to take her along. A bad choice, if I may be permitted to say so.

Poor Franz. Can't hide his resentment. His left cheek starts to twitch with boundless jealousy of Mrs. Q. A bad choice, he repeats. May I help you with your coat?

He takes my coat, hangs it on a hanger and hangs the hanger on a hook in the wall. I watch his methodical tactics with rising concern. The gun in the inside pocket—did he notice?

I sit down at the table in view of the coat while Franz serves me a passable meal from Father's leftovers. No liquor. Not even wine? But Franz pretends he doesn't have the keys to the cellar. However, he will be glad to share the beer he keeps in reserve in his rooms.

He's marched off to fetch the beer. Did Father leave on business or for a rest? I imagine him on a secluded islet, briefcase and phone by his side in the coral sand. Mrs. Q, pink in a flutter of pink flamingos, is kneeling over him, massaging his brown back. I would have done a more efficient job on him. But here is Franz with the beer.

A glass, sir.

No thanks. I'll drink from the can.

Yes, sir, it is more practical.

He returns the glasses to the cabinet and raises the can to his thin lips.

Not much of a drinking man, our loyal Franz. Half a can and he gets woozy. Sings I don't know what—Die Lorelei? Downs the rest, squashes the can in his big-knuckled fist, and his jealousy of Mrs. Q breaks to the fore. A middle-aged overweight society lady—how on earth will she protect the chief? Any seeing eye dog would be more useful. If I care to hear his opinion, a famous personality like the chief must never travel without a combat trained bodyguard.

The world is not secure like it was in my days, muses our Franz. Then we had law and order. Today it's all muggings and murders and commie kidnappers abroad.

Abroad? Aha. So Father went abroad. To what country? Come on, Franz. Be a nice guy. You can tell me. I'm still his son.

Sorry, sir. I have strict orders. I can't.

You can go to hell!

I'm on my feet. Exasperated, I lunge for my coat and the gun drops onto the floor with a clatter. I pick it up, conscious how he is on instant alert, eyes fixed on the weapon, body positioned to jump me, lips parting slowly in disbelief as I pass him the gun muzzle down.

Just turn it over to my father whenever he's back from wherever he is or isn't. Say, man, you didn't really think I'd shoot you dead for a fuckin address!

There's always that possibility, sir.

He weighs the pistol on his palm. A nicely balanced piece. Would fit into a lady's purse. He pulls the slide back and smirks. You know, sir, it isn't loaded?

What did you think? Of course I know, I lie as I make a hasty exit from the kitchen, rid of the gun but still in total darkness as to my old man's whereabouts.

•

But God, the ferocious glare in the vestibule! It stuns you, blinds you. If nothing else, at least the light used to be soft in this circular entrance hall of pure white marble. Why the sudden waste of electricity—to keep the bad guys out? I ask myself, trapped in the glare as though the cops were shining the lamp on me in one of those old precinct houses, the last of the grand old marble structures our city fathers haven't demolished yet.

I don my shades. One thing's for sure: Con Ed is making a fortune on my old man—provided he doesn't already own Con Ed, I reconsider as I linger, oddly disappointed that his voice isn't bouncing back at me from one of the rooms which fan out in stately procession, each growing smaller as it recedes in space...
    smaller...
        smaller...

•

Why, daddy?
An optical illusion, James.
He towered above me, his formal dress the only blackness in a white sea of marble. They were ready to leave for a dinner party. Mother, sheathed in low-cut

sleek green silk, came down the stairs and seated herself in an oval niche between two sirens. She bent down and removed her left slipper. It was greener than her dress. She waved at me with the slipper and shook a pebble out of it—*ping*. I grinned and waved back.

An optical illusion. Father frowned at his watch. I must ask you not to dawdle, he warned her across empty space. We are running late.

I'm ready, honey. I'll wait for you in the car. She darted by me, green and slim. She blew me a kiss and was gone.

Perspective. The system behind the illusion. I'll explain, but I must be brief. So pay attention.

Yes, daddy.

I piously folded my hands. But the assumption of linear perspective was lost on me. My eyes had strayed to Mother's purse. It was still lying on the bench, green and forgotten. The moment Father had done with perspective, I would run to the car with her little green purse and earn myself a thank-you hug and a big kiss.

•

Put it back where you found it, James.

Why, daddy? Mommy needs it.

I said put it back. NOW. His command rolled through the vestibule like cannon fire. He snatched the purse from me, flung it back on the bench, and with a "damned scatterbrained female" strode out.

I fondled the castaway purse. I licked the tiny butterflies embroidered in seed pearls. I undid the clasp to sniff the rosy interior when she came flying back into the vestibule, her long red hair a wilderness, her dress half torn.

What happened, mommy?

She didn't answer. She wouldn't even look at me. She grabbed the purse, clutched it to her breasts and dashed out. In seconds I heard the splatter of gravel as the car left the driveway.

It pulled out so fast, I still don't understand how she made it inside before the door slammed shut on her. Who had been driving—the chauffeur or father? I don't recall. But I do recall an incident many years later when a spike heel broke off her shoe and she had to run after the car with one foot bare. At that time, I'm certain, my old man was at the wheel.

•

The vestibule a frozen pond, smooth and transparent. Fish with human faces flit under the ice. Enters Franz in the uniform of an American soldier. Snaps to attention. Salutes.

One stolen weapon recaptured.

Hands me a rifle. I spin around and shoot into a corridor of endless rooms. I shoot through windows, mirrors. I shoot down all the crystal chandeliers. Father is applauding in a blizzard of shattered glass.

Not bad for a first try, sonny. Try again.

Is he hiding in the library behind the books? I can't see him.

Go for it! Aim!

I can't. Where am I, daddy?

The ice is giving under my boots. My mouth fills with mud. I'm sinking.

Daddy! Daddy!

•

A dream. You aren't surprised. But imagine my surprise to hear myself, a grown man, scream for daddy as I wake up on Mother's soft divan to the drip drop of icicles melting, roused by my scream or by the sun in the stained glass window of Art Nouveau vegetation and frolicking sprites. Daddy! Daddy! And I was no longer dreaming.

Freud lurking in the wings? But that is only one minutia of a puzzle I must leave for you to solve or forget. I can't do either. I'm too involved. I am part of the script.

So here I was in Mother's memorable boudoir. The laurel branch she kept on the mantle was gone. Otherwise little had changed. I shook myself free of my dream and my clothes, eager for a long, luxurious bath. But when I opened the faucet, the water from the ancient pipes ran thick and rusty. Her tub had not been used in months.

I pulled the stopper and watched the water drain with a labored gulp. When had I last been to her quarters? Not since her death. Not even on the day of her wake when her ghost danced through the armory amid flowers and bridal ribbons. But of course she was dead.

Her door has fallen shut behind me. I'm out of the house and hold on to my cap in a quick, capricious wind.

•

The overnight thaw has transfigured the park into a liquid mirage. I've cranked the cab window down as the world flows by in a mauve, luminous haze. But the cabby's fez is clearly defined in space: a static form, even though the cab proceeds in fits and starts through slush and traffic. It is a battered, antiquated cab. But the cabby, honking long and with abundance, is young indeed.

We stop at a light and he flashes me a smile. Black curls spring up from under his red fez. His skin is brown and shiny.

Nice morning.

A very beautiful morning, I say with conviction.

Very beautiful your country America.

Very beautiful that fez you're wearing. Turkish?

Arab. No way no fez in Turkey.

So we talk on in counterpoint, not always sure what the other tries to convey. But I untangle the essentials. Seems he drove some Arabs up Queens Boulevard. Found the fez on the backseat early this morning. Tried it on for fun and kept it on. But he's a Turk.

He comes from a small fishing village. His baby son and wife have stayed behind. He'll soon bring them over—as soon as he's saved up enough money. He'd also send for his old papa and mama. But they don't trust America. They'll stay in Antalya.

Antalya? The name rings a bell!

No way! The cabby shakes his head emphatically. No bells no way in Antalya.

•

No bells no way, not in that isolated, coastal strip my old man had picked for his operational base and where I found myself immobilized within the savage beauty of rocks and sea—a prisoner of my own making. For I had done my utmost to sweet talk him into having me for a travel companion. He had not cherished the idea.

He routinely traveled alone and I realized it would be difficult to change his mind. But I was seventeen and it was spring. The dogwood trees behind the house had broken into frothy white blossoms. I had graduated from Hitchcock's—free at last yet at loose ends. Expected to stay put and prepare for college, yet burning to see the world. Turkey was on top of my list. A recent slide show of that extraordinary land had reawakened an old childhood fantasy of adventure.

He met me in the library and I lost no time to work on him. I begged and cajoled. I shamelessly sucked up to his ego. A trip in his creative company! It would be an inspiration, a character builder! An education tantamount to a lifetime spent at his alma mater!

That did the trick. He shot me one of his skeptical looks but gave in, though not before I'd sworn that I'd make no demands on his time.

I'm leaving on a highly sensitive mission. The success of a crucial deal will depend on my peace of mind, my absolute privacy. Is that understood?

Yes, Father.

A breeze came drifting through the open window whose arch framed a cut of the night: a slim crescent moon on a gun-metal blue sky. Hadn't I seen an almost identical cut at the slide show? The recognition gave me a jolt. For I'd heard on yesterday's news that the photographer turned out to be a double agent who had his cover blown inside a mosque. His chopped-off head was discovered in Antalya in the rubble of an archaeological dig.

I cringed. You'll have your privacy, sir! I won't be in your way, I promised.

Well then, get cracking. Get packed. We'll be leaving early.

So at an ungodly hour the following morning we were airborne for Antalya—the only passengers, seated far apart from one another in the giant belly of the corporate jet.

•

No press or tourists spoiled my old man's privacy, no noisy traffic or kids. Our modest inn stood off the beaten path amid sheer cliffs, high above a gold-blue Mediterranean. The innkeepers, a quiet, elderly couple, spoke no English. The only human under thirty was a deaf-mute baby girl who sat tied to her chair on the front porch, her round, observant eyes scanning a wilderness of distant gray-purple mountains. I'd sit alongside, voiceless like she, my eyes like hers on the inaccessible mountain chain beyond the bay. Below the porch, the wash would flap on the line in the wind in a drowsy smell of juniper and hay. Someone would shout. The donkey in the yard would bray. And suddenly these sounds would cease and I could hear the solitude around us.

We were immersed in solitude. But my old man was restless. He'd rummage about long before the muezzin's call for morning prayer rose through the mist in the valley. His steps in the adjoining room would wake me up, and unlatching the wooden shutters, I'd watch him mount the donkey in the yard. A tall black cutout under the stars, he'd ride down the serpentine path, his flashlight dipping from sight behind the juniper thicket. He was on his way to catch the first bus into town. That much he had told me.

What was he doing in the crumbling harbor town of fallen towers and deadened alleys? He wouldn't say. We rarely spoke. Sharing an occasional meal in the near-empty dining room, he might ask me to pass him the pepper which he'd copiously pour on his mutton, not saying another word.

So he continued taciturn and glum. Until one blazing noon I heard him whistle Yankee Doodle from afar as he came riding up the path and emerged in the sun drenched yard a changed man. All smiles he dismounted and spread out his arms, to embrace me I imagined. But he embraced the donkey.

Good girl. He patted her rump. You brought me luck.

For he had clinched the deal, had won the battle. The coveted Grecian helmet with a chunk of human skull stuck in the bronze—it was his, it was on his back. In his field pack.

A victory against all odds. A find in a million. His self-congratulations caught in the grimy light of the stairs as he bounded up ahead of me two steps at a time.

Strange, with the trophy bulging from his back he looked like a hunchback. The thought came and went. He had stepped into the shuttered privacy of his room. I went to mine.

●

I had dozed off in the noonday heat, my face in a skin magazine I'd salvaged from under the stairs, when three loud thumps against the partition wall knocked me out of bed. Father had signaled. I stuck my head into the water bucket. And dripping wet with my shorts inside out I scrambled to obey the royal summons. A waste of energy. I might as well have slept the day away.

Oblivious of the world or me, he stood in the open window in a swimming blue of sky and sea. I squinted into the glare. Was he cradling a football against his bare chest? Hell, no. It was the helmet. He slowly raised it level with his eyes and, frowning, scrutinized the round of embossment. It was a mythological scene. But what did it represent—a sacrificial ritual? A wedding?

Could the harp be a rib cage? The amphora a torso? The drinking bowl a severed head? Ho James.

At last he had caught sight of me in the mirror of the old armoire.

The outside needs work, he said offhand into the mirror. However, the inside is in superb condition. Superb.

His voice gained fire. He swung around and faced me directly. A chunk of the cranium, incredibly well preserved through the millenniums! Here, have a look.

The helmet veered above my head. He'll have me try it on for size, I thought. And though I knew that such an asinine joke wouldn't occur to my old man in time or space, the sheer idea of a dead guy's skull touching mine...and this guy was deader than dead... Yuck. I coulda puked.

A beauty, eh! My revulsion had passed him by. He lovingly carried his prize to a nook in the thick white-washed wall. And jingling some coins, left over from his clandestine bus trips to town, he cried out in orgiastic ecstasy: This merits a celebration. How do we feel about a cup of local wine?

•

I loathe his monarchical WE. What about me? Why should I celebrate his rotten skull bone? Fuck your helmet, daddy. You can stuff it.

He pours out two cups, hands me mine with an arrogant caveat—sip, don't gulp, this vintage is heady stuff—and takes his cup to the window. Whereupon I gleefully drink mine down at one gulp and pour myself another one. Father in the window hugs his knees and gazes out at a fishing fleet that is scrawled on the crazy blue mirror sea. I keep hitting the bottle.

Sure heady stuff. Head's gone wavy. Wavy helmet split in wavy wall. Water mirror buckling, cracking. Fishing fleet drowned in blue mist. Old man in the window a spidery cartoon. Hi, dad!

I turn my empty bottle upside down and lull I'd love to watch him drink from the helmet like those male manly heroes he read me about a trillion foggy light years back in time. Helmet fancy cup of cheers. Fancy piss-pot...

I'm fumbling for his trophy and am blocked by his fist. You drunken idiot!

I hear no more. I wet my pants and pass out cold at his feet.

•

My old man finagled to ship his treasure by diplomatic pouch to the U.S. and my sins were forgiven. Let bygones be bygones. Tomorrow we'd be flying home. We might as well use our final day together and explore the coastline, he proposed.

So we hiked up the winding shore past crags and crevices, most likely over buried Hittite remnants, he explained. Yesterday on his way back from town he'd stopped by a new site where some significant fragments of Hittite sculpture were being dug up. He'd briefly engaged two students in shoptalk—one of them from Ankara U., the other from Champaign, Illinois. Delightful chaps. If we weren't short of time, he'd ask them over for dinner.

And when might that be? But he had already taken off backwards in time to land with the Hittites whose monumental works in stone were the glorious legacy of ruthless invaders. Or had he said toothless investors? The sudden roar of a fighter plane was mangling his words.

One of ours. From the nearby air force base, he observed, back in the here and now. The plane nosedived beyond a silver horizon as we climbed a steep trail. I lagged behind. He had already reached the summit. I saw him stand alarmingly close to the edge of the overhanging cliff, bent down to appraise the height; while I, a chronic sufferer of acrophobia, peered wearily through the tent of his legs into a fathomless chasm.

I take it you are an adequate diver, said Father and dropped his pants, standing stark naked above me and minus his testicles.

I'd rather not swim in the nude, dad… In my funk I'd failed to notice his jockstrap.

You wear underdrawers, don't you? Well then, what's keeping you?

He'd balanced himself on the edge of the shelf. And down he streaked through space in a faultless swan dive.

Good bye, sweet world. I shut my eyes. I pinched my nose and hurled myself into my wat'ry grave. But I lived and the devil in me was more than alive as I pretended to be drowning; going under, surfacing, thrashing the waves. Screaming Help! and going under again though this time I had no strength left to force myself up. I had played the drowning game too well.

But it worked! He came to my rescue. He swam me to the nearest shore and laid me out on the gravelly beach which was much nearer than I had expected. I furtively squinted through one eye and saw the wash on the line and the innkeeper feeding the chickens.

Jimmy! Are you alright?

He tore off my T-shirt and was listening to my heart. Jimmy! Answer me! Jimmy!

I'm OK, dad. I heard him exhale.

Thank God. You gave me the scare of my life.

So there. He cared. He really cared. I bit my lips to hide my satisfaction. Would we have to climb back to the summit to retrieve our things?

No time. Some locals will find them and use them. Always remember, James, this country is dirt poor, no matter how many billions we're pouring in.

•

Yours is a beautiful country, I say to the cabby.

Very beautiful. Very poor. He's saving up his money to buy the taxi and go to Turkey.

Go to Turkey by taxi?

This breaks him up. To Turkey and back to America with wife and baby son in his own taxi! The joke overwhelms him. He nearly collides with a garbage truck as he backs into a filling station.

Dirty Arab! yells the driver.

Very beautiful your country. Fill her up.

The sun is in my eyes and I reach for my shades. But these aren't mine. They are Father's dark glasses. I must have picked them up when I left Mother's place this morning.

I shut my eyes. And leaning back, I see him grope his way through the maze of her room in stippled multicolored patterns of light and shadow. He takes off his glasses and, one arm flung over his eyes, falls asleep on her couch below the tall window of inexhaustible dreams.

•

We've made it to my neighborhood. The cabby is navigating a major puddle, and shit and slush fly up against our windshield. He curses in Turkish, brakes and jumps out. Picks up a rock and with another potent curse hurls it into the puddle. But when he cleans the windshield, his patience is endless. He soaps, scrapes, rinses, polishes until the glass sparkles. One day the taxi will be his. He stoops and washes first the rag and then his hands in a mound of melting snow.

I've climbed out behind him. Stocky, handsome kid. Trim ass and legs. Spatular, capable fingers. A fisherman from Antalya's harsh coast. I ought to visit there again—live there perhaps? Forget the shipwrecks on Clone Island? Explore Asia Minor? Learn how to work in stone?

I impulsively pull out my wallet and hand him a large bill. For your taxi to Turkey.

Ah...beautiful.... He contemplates the gift in mystical awe. Americans beautiful people. He presses the bill to his lips, then sticks it into his Levis and scribbles his uncle's phone number in Flushing, Queens on the inside of a Wrigley's chewing gum wrapper.

You want taxi, I drive. On that we shake hands.

Should I risk an embrace? But his arms have already opened wide for a hug and a kiss on both cheeks. Then he's back in his cab and sails off.

Tesekkür ederim! It's Turkish for thank you, and I yell it into a bedlam of belching trucks and honking horns and wailing sirens. I yell and wave my lucky cap as the taxi pitches, rolls and dissolves in a watery distance. But the fez remains fixed in my mind—a red truncated cone whose afterimage follows me as I wade the few steps to my building.

•

The frozen stream melted during the night and left the beat-up pavement a shimmering map of floating islands, rivulets and iridescent puddles. Atop my stoop the neighbor's cat is preening herself in the sun and from Paddy's comes an enticing whiff of Irish stew, their Monday special. Before I head home and clean up the mess in my loft, I'll treat myself to a belated lunch.

Few customers at Paddy's at this hour. Behind the half empty bar, my good friend Jimmy is busy checking the Racing Form.

Hi there! He's glancing up. How was your Sunday?

Not bad, I say as I struggle out of my storm coat when something bumps against my ribs—the gun! While I was fast asleep on Mother's couch, dreaming up a blizzard and crying for daddy, Franz must have crept into the room commando style and spirited the weapon back into my pocket.

I shake my head, bemused but not surprised.

What can I do for you? Jimmy puts the Racing Form aside and our faces merge in the flecked mirror.

Thank you, Jimmy. The usual. Straight up. And make it a double.